THE RHYTHM OF YOUR HEART!

XO CAP

TRAVEL WITH ME & SEE

NEW YORK

Oh hey, Explorers!
Ready to join me in NYC?
Check out my music–
Follow along and sing with me!

♥ B

free download

Scan with your phone!

New York, New York
(feat. Gabrielle Waters)
Travel With Me & See

*Visit travelwithmeandsee.com
to explore more!*

New York, New York ♥

NEW YORKERS,

Thank you for your magic. The energy from NYC inspires children from all over the world to believe in themselves and the power they have to chase their dreams.

Nancy Delevoye
CARLY GRIMES

Special thanks to:

Amy Allen   Jeff Allen   Jessixa Bagley   Karin Baugher   Christopher Bevans   Chris Cabanillas
Abe Donner   Kelly Davis   Amanda Pearl   Jaclyn Brown   Jennifer Smid   Chloe Rhodes
Johanne S. Vanderbeek   Lindsey Maliekel   Sara Cataldo   Tracy Scotto Rinaldi   Emily Blythe Kerrigan
Fred Vosloh   Lauren Wiggins   Derek Wiggins   Morgan Zion   & in loving memory of Maggie Keith.

Text Copyright © 2020 by Nancy Delevoye
Illustrations Copyright © 2020 by Carly Grimes
Music Copyright © 2020 Travel With Me & See with Gabrielle Waters
All rights reserved. No part of this book may be reproduced,
transmitted or stored in an information retreival system in any form or by any means,
graphic, electronic or mechanical, including photocopying, taping and recording,
without prior written permission from the publishers.
First edition printed 2021.
First copy edit by Kim Dunavent
ISBN 978-0-9600423-3-3 (hardcover, 8.5x11)
This book was typeset in American Typewriter.
The illustrations were done with watercolor pencil, markers & ink.
Self-published by Nancy Delevoye and Carly Grimes. Seattle, WA, USA.

*Visit travelwithmeandsee.com
to explore more!*

TRAVEL WITH ME & SEE

NEW YORK

INDEX

New Yorkers

Alicia Keys - Grammy® Award-winning singer/songwriter/producer who began piano lessons at seven years old and composing music at age 14! Just two years later she graduated as valedictorian from the Professional Performing Arts School in Manhattan.

Frank Sinatra - Born to Italian Sicilian immigrants (1915-1998), he is considered one of the greatest musicians of the 20th century. Frank Sinatra was not only an award-winning singer, he was also an award-winning film actor.

Immigrant - One who moves to a new country to live permanently.

Rockettes - The Radio City Rockettes perform a mix of tap, jazz, modern dance and ballet. Each show has 36 coordinated dancers that will perform eye-high kicks - sometimes up to 300 kicks per show!

On the Map

Bronx - The greenest borough in the city, which includes the Bronx Zoo. The Bronx is also the birthplace of hip hop, and is also home to the New York Yankees.

Brooklyn - Home to DUMBO (not the elephant), where you can shop, eat and ride a carousel under the Brooklyn Bridge.

Five Boroughs - The five "districts" of NYC: The Bronx, Brooklyn, Manhattan, Queens, and Staten Island.

Harlem - Original habitants were Native Americans named Manhattan. Today Harlem is best known for its Black American art and culture, and especially its jazz music!

Manhattan - Think lots and lots of skyscrapers located on an island. Manhattan is considered to be the heart of the Big Apple.

New York City - NYC. The most populous city in the United States and the first American home town for many immigrants.

Queens - While Queens is home to the Mets, we want to tell you about the Queens of the court - the tennis court! The U.S. Open is held in Queens, a tournmament that both Serena Williams and Billie Jean King won many times, thus in our eyes making them the Queens of Queens!

Staten Island - Take a ride on the FREE Staten Island Ferry as the views of Manhattan will delight you! Staten Island is the only borough separated from the rest of NY by water (The New York Bay).

Nicknames

Ads - Short for advertisements.

Big Apple - Nickname for New York City.

Empire State - Nickname for New York State.

New Yorkers - Persons who were born, or who are living in New York.

Land of the Free - A phrase in the U.S. national anthem, that later created the nickname for the United States.   4

Must See

Broadway - (Broadway Theatre) Refers to the theatrical performances by 41 professional theatres.

Brooklyn Bridge - Connects Brooklyn to Manhattan over the East River. Circus showman, P.T. Barnum, once took 21 elephants over the bridge to show how safe the bridge was.

Central Park - The first public park built in America and the most visited urban park in the United States. Most of the bedrock in the park was formed by glaciers millions of years ago!

Fearless Girl - A bronze sculpture of a young girl by artist, Kristen Visbal. An original plaque read, "Know the power of women in leadership. SHE makes a difference."

9/11 Memorial & Museum - Dedicated to those who lost their lives, and the heroes who helped, in the September 11th Terrorist attack on Twin Towers.

New York Stock Exchange - In simple terms, a market where people can buy and sell shares (representing ownership) of a company that is looking to raise money so it can grow bigger.

Radio City Music Hall - Home to the Rockettes, it also is a venue that holds live concerts and events.

Rockefeller Center - Be on the lookout for someone famous walking around! Rockefeller is also home to the news stations and live talk shows, which often have famous guest stars.

Statue of Liberty - The lady of liberty was a gift from France in 1886 and was shipped to America in 300 pieces in 214 crates across the Atlantic Ocean.

Thanksgiving Parade - Fun fact - each giant helium balloon requires 50 to 90 people to keep it from flying away into the air!

Times Square - With 55 giant LED displays, it shines so brightly that it can be seen from outer space.

Music

My Way - Frank Sinatra made this song quite famous. The little mouse, Mike, in the movie Sing, also performs this song as his final act!

New York, New York - Lyrics and vocals by Gabrielle Waters, written specially for this book! Download it on iTunes, Amazon Music, Spotify or YouTube Music to sing along.

This Land is Your Land - One of the USA's most famous folk songs, written by Woodie Guthrie.

Uptown Girl - Written and performed by New York's own, Billy Joel.

Showbiz

Audition - An interview for a role or job as a singer, actor, dancer or musician.

Broadcasting - Transmission of programs or information by radio or television.

Debut - verb. To perform in public for the first time.

Stage fright - Nervousness before or during an appearance in front of an audience.

Standing ovation - An extra long clapping (and sometimes cheering) by a crowd or audience that has risen to their feet during or following a performance.

Explorers!

I want to start with a little history today,
about people who ventured to the **U.S.of A**.

1892 - 1954
Over 12 million people entered
the United States via Ellis Island.
The Statue of Liberty stands there and
was often the first thing immigrants
saw when arriving by boat.
Many were fleeing famine, drought,
war or political oppression.

PACIFIC
OCEAN

INDIAN
OCEAN

TIC
AN

Brave **immigrants** traveled by boat
across the stormy sea.
For a much better life,
they sought the **land of the free**.

Having packed up their dreams,
they carried hope in their hearts.
New York City promised
a brand new start.

High in the sky,
greeting them upon arrival
was the **Statue of Liberty**.
She made them smile.

To all the hungry and tired masses,
let your hearts roam free.
Here we welcome your hope and dreams.
This land was made for you and me.

9

New arrivals settled in one of the **Five Boroughs**:
Manhattan, Staten Island, The Bronx, Brooklyn, and Queens.

Such different neighborhoods
with their own unique scenes.

New York's magic also
inspired the children to go far.
The son of Sicilian **immigrants**
became a bona fide star.

Frank Sinatra sang, danced,
and performed on **Broadway**.
He also starred in movies.
He did it all...and in his own way!

The city offered so much to do.
Some things old, and some things new.

Like watching the **Thanksgiving Day Parade**,
with its giant balloons in the air that swayed.

Or holiday ice-skating
at **Rockefeller Center**–
a treasured tradition
during the month of December.

Wow! That sounds sooooo magical!

MEMORY LANE

New York is where we stand today,
inspired by dreamers, who keep paving the way.

Firefighters, police officers,
ball players and well-dressed bankers.
Fancy dancers, artists extraordinaire,
and the fashionistas deciding what to wear.

Doctors, professors,
and Broadway actors.
Politicians,
great musicians,
and top chefs cooking
in their kitchens.

All dreamers with ambition.

We, too, have a dream
and the **Big Apple** is daring us to take a bite.
Will it be sour or sweet?
Rotten or ripe?

What is our dream?
You might want to know?
It is for me to sing,
while Little Dove plays piano.

Follow along, as we make our **debut**.
Empire State, we are coming for you!

Starting out on the **Brooklyn Bridge**
we jog towards **Manhattan**.
Excited by the possibility,
that anything can happen.

We run into **Fearless Girl**
at the **New York Stock Exchange**.
She tells us we are powerful
and can influence important change.

Visiting the **9/11 Memorial & Museum**,
we stop to pause and reflect.
These brave hearts we remember,
with honor and respect.

The wind starts to blow
and we continue on our way.
Headed for the bright lights
of the shows on **Broadway**!

At a **Broadway** theatre
we greet the doorman and say,

"Hello, sir. We'd like the opportunity
to sing in your musical play."

He laughingly replies,
"Showbiz is a game.
Some spend their whole lives
trying to make it to fame!

You'll need an agent,
perhaps a fancy name.
You'll need to **audition**,
to play in this game.

I wouldn't waste any more time here.
Head over to the famous **Times Square**."

He promptly shuts the door in our face.
Little Dove sighs, "Not the right place."

Times Square shines so bright,
we almost forget that it is night.

Little Dove suggests "Let's buy a hot dog from a street vendor
and soak in the Ads displayed with such splendor.

There are electric billboards for
some of the most famous Broadway shows:
Hamilton, Wickod, Tho Lion King,
and whooaaah....

Do you see that?
The Talented Underdog Ad?"

Singers, songwriters and musicians—
this is your chance to shine at **auditions**.

A select few will advance to perform,
broadcasting live, across every platform!

Early morning in **Central Park**,
the birds are chirping away.
The rocks are also calling out,
"Come over to climb and play!"

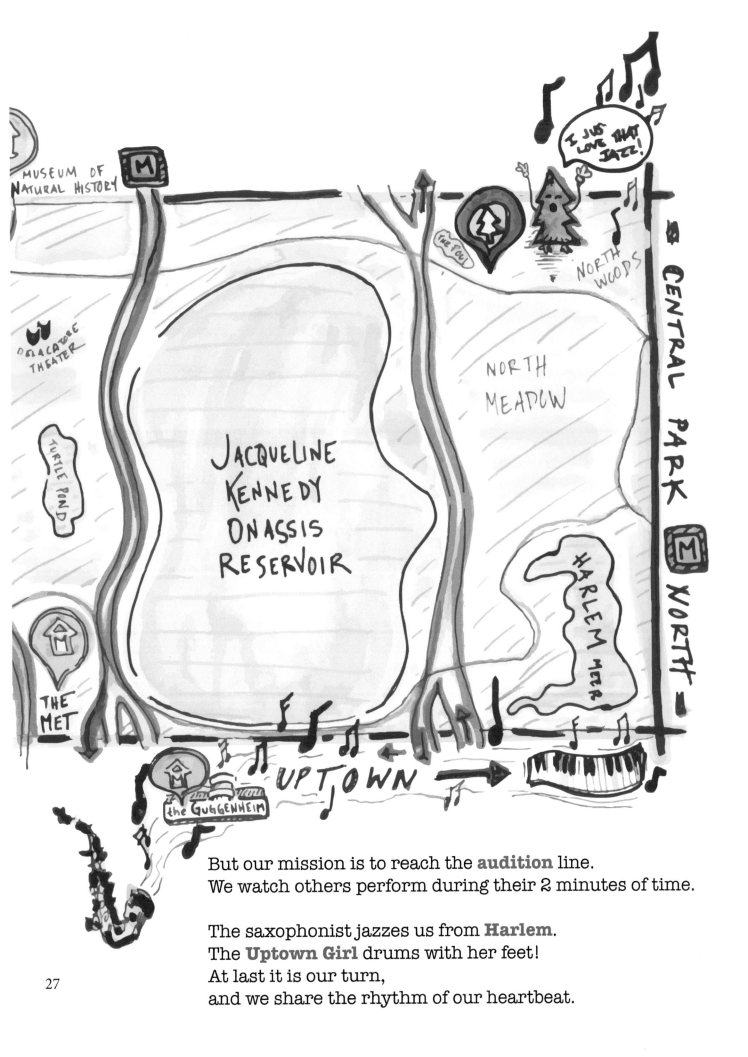

But our mission is to reach the **audition** line.
We watch others perform during their 2 minutes of time.

The saxophonist jazzes us from **Harlem**.
The **Uptown Girl** drums with her feet!
At last it is our turn,
and we share the rhythm of our heartbeat.

Our **audition** ends
and now we must wait.
It's up to the judges
to determine our fate.

Little Dove says in a tired voice,
"B, we gave it our best!
Let's find lunch
and a place to rest."

With cream cheese dripping from his beak
Little Dove tries to speak:

"Rolled, boiled and baked,
these New York Bagels take the cake!
Add some jelly, perhaps a fluffy egg and bacon.
Toppings are limitless with imagination...."

I interrupt him with a squeal,
"**WE MADE IT!** Our dream is becoming **REAL!**

We received the notification
that we will sing live for the entire nation!"

It's Saturday night at
Radio City Music Hall.
Butterflies dance in our stomachs
as we prepare to give it our all.

Backstage the **Rockettes**
move by us with precision.
Their centipede legs
walk in perfect unison.

Walking out on stage,
the lights blind our eyes.
We take a deep breath and let out

one,

last,

sigh...

We sing and play our hearts away.
Our feet move to the rhythm by tapping.
There is cheering from the crowd
as they wildly start clapping!

The crowd gives us a **standing ovation**
and **Alicia Keys** appears on stage.
She, too, had a dream to play music
from a very young age.

Alicia takes the mic,
"It is without a doubt that we have our winners!
Congratulations Little Dove and B —
you've made your **debut** as heartfelt singers!"

We feel a gratitude
that is hard to express,
and thank everyone
for the magic they possess.

"Our journey of dreams has only just started...

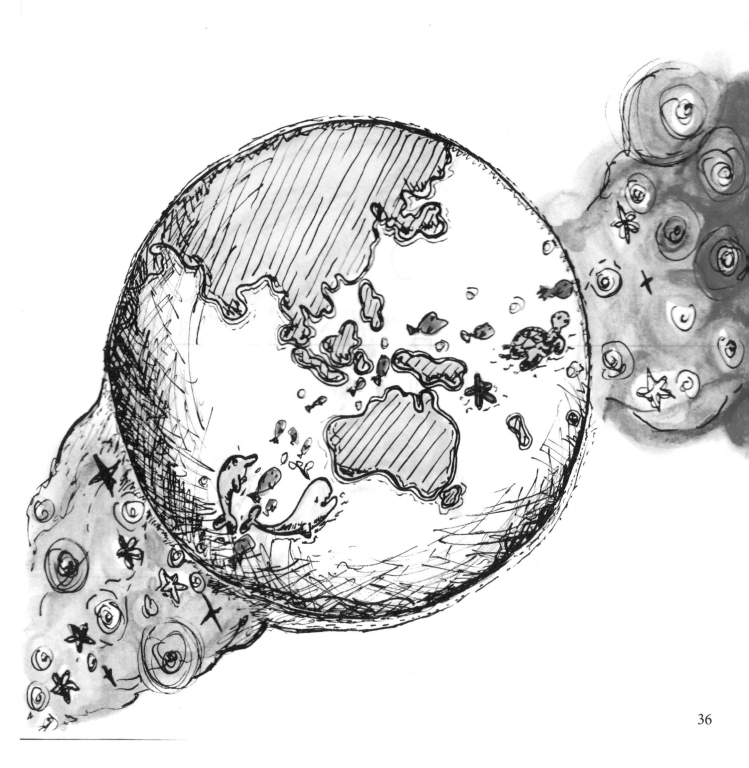

there is still so much that remains **uncharted**."

TRAVEL WITH ME & SEE

Explorers!

Thank you for joining me in NYC.
Where should Little Dove & I go next?
I have some ideas,
but I really want to hear from you!

Email connect@travelwithmeandsee.com
Instagram @travelwithmeandsee.kids
Twitter @AdventuresWithB
YouTube Travel With Me & See

Travel With Me & See Paris
ISBN: 978-0-9600423-1-9

Travel With Me & See London
ISBN: 978-0-9600423-2-6

Travel With Me & See New York
ISBN: 978-0-9600423-3-3

*Visit travelwithmeandsee.com
to explore more!*

CPSIA information can be obtained
at www.ICGtesting.com
Printed in the USA
BVHW020921080221
598828BV00003B/4